Ann has always enjoyed books and reading, preferring to escape into an imaginary world. This is something she has passed on to both of her children. Ann's enthusiasm for books has inspired many aspects of her work, especially in her prior career as both a Primary and SEN teacher. She enjoys sharing books and stories at home, and previously at school. Ann used pictures she drew in her son's bedroom to inspire her sealife characters.

Ann Graves

Olly Octopus
Shares a Smile

AUSTIN MACAULEY PUBLISHERS™

LONDON • CAMBRIDGE • NEW YORK • SHARJAH

Copyright © Ann Graves (2019)

A CIP catalogue record for this title is available from the British Library.

ISBN 9781788481700 (Paperback)
ISBN 9781788481717 (E-Book)
www.austinmacauley.com

First Published (2019)
Austin Macauley Publishers Ltd
25 Canada Square
Canary Wharf
London
E14 5LQ

This book is dedicated to Wiggles and Bear –
don't stop dreaming.

Thank you to all my family for their support but especially Gravey, without you this would never have happened. Also, Mum and Dad, for your constant encouragement.

The warm sun shone on the shiny turquoise sea. The rays danced down through the clear blue water. Seaweed swirled as fish swam by.

Down deep at the bottom of the sea, under a reef of bright coral, lived an octopus.

A little yellow octopus, with a splattering of orange spots and extremely long tentacles, called Olly.

Olly was fast asleep, small bubbles rising and popping as he snored softly. His eight long tentacles curled around his blobby body.

The ends of his tentacles twitched as he dreamt of the mischievous things he'd got up to the day before.

Waking with a start, his long tentacles unfurled, stretching along the seabed.

Olly was hungry.

Reaching out two of his extremely long tentacles high above and feeling along the edge of the reef, he picked up a couple of clams.

Munching on his find, Olly peered out of his cave.

"Today will be full of fun," he smiled.

Wriggling out of his cave, Olly scooted through the deep cool water looking for someone who needed a smile.

Soon, Olly spotted a shoal of
shiny silver fish.

Looking around to check he hadn't been
spotted, Olly quickly hid behind a bunch
of glossy seaweed.

He watched as the fish swam together,
back and forth, as one. All of them
following the lead fish, round and round
and up and down.

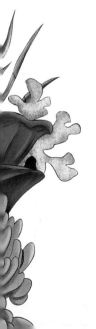

Watching them move, shimmering in the sun's rays, Olly's tentacles twitched.

Slowly, he allowed one tentacle to stretch out, waiting for the group to swim past again.

As they did, Olly tickled the lead fish, who darted away in surprise. All of the fish swished off in their own directions before circling round to form a group once more.

Olly chuckled to himself as he waited for a chance to do it again. This time, he tickled the lead fish and several followers, using all his tentacles.

Soon the fish were scattered, bubbles rising rapidly as they giggled. "Stop! Stop!" they chorused.

After a while, Olly gave one last tickle, hoping he had managed to get each fish at least once. He pulled back his long tentacles.

Moving away with a smile, Olly went on his way, looking for more mischief.

Soon, Olly was causing cheerful
chuckles all over the seabed.

He tickled a gloomy looking pufferfish.
Causing it to puff up repeatedly, until it
was laughing too hard to deflate again.

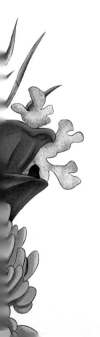

Olly tickled Sammi, a great white shark, who was patrolling around the reef for something to eat.

The shark's tail swished wildly as he chortled deeply, giving all the smaller fish a chance to hide.

Charlie, a chuckling clownfish, returned
to hide in his anemone each time Olly's
twitching tentacles tickled
his stripy belly.

To add to his fun, on his return journey
to his cave, Olly managed to tickle...

an eel

a dog fish

and a blue whale.

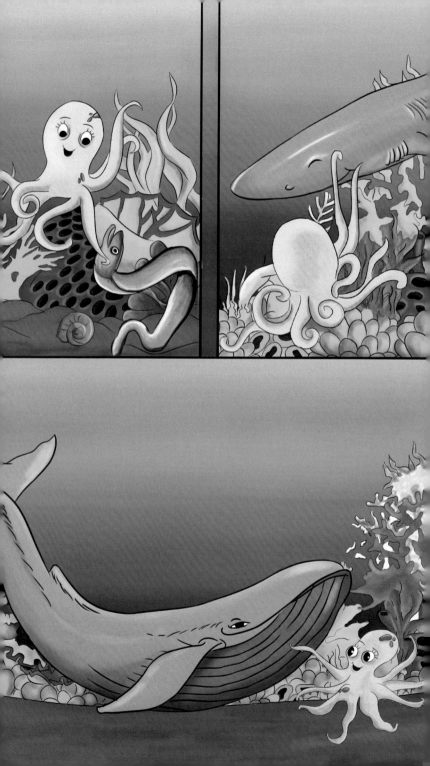

Olly even tickled a grumpy old stingray,
causing him to flap clouds of sand
in several directions.

Wriggling back into his dark cave,
Olly was happy with his day's
fun and frolics.

He smiled to himself as he thought about
the laughter he had created.

So next time you are paddling in the sea, and you feel something tickle your toes.

Look down carefully to see.

Perhaps, it's a stray strand of seaweed.

Or maybe, just maybe, Olly is hiding nearby, stretching out his long tentacles...

making sure you have a smile on your face too.